British Library Cataloguing in Publication Data
Willis, Jeanne
  Dr. Xargle's book of earth hounds.
  I. Pets: dogs
  I. Title II. Ross, Tony, *1938-*
  636.7

ISBN 0-86264-249-3

First published in Great Britain in 1989 by Andersen Press Ltd., 20 Vauxhall Bridge Road,
London SW1V 2SA. Published in Australia by Random House Australia Pty. Ltd.,
20 Alfred Street, Milsons Point, Sydney NSW 2061. All rights reserved.
Colour separated by Photolitho AG Offsetreproduktionen, Gossau, Zürich, Switzerland.
Printed and bound in Italy by Grafiche AZ, Verona.

4 5 6 7 8 9

DR XARGLE'S
BOOK OF
EARTH HOUNDS

Translated into Human by Jeanne Willis
Pictures by Tony Ross

Andersen Press · London

Good morning, class.

Today we are going to learn about Earth Hounds.

Earth Hounds have fangs at the front and a waggler at the back.

To find out which is which, hold a sausage at both ends.

Earth Hounds have buttons for eyes, a sniffer with
two holes in and a long, pink flannel.

With the pink flannel they lick their
undercarriages,

frogs which are deceased and the icicles of
Earthlets who are not looking.

Earth Hounds can stand on four legs, three legs and two legs. They can jump as high as a roast beef.

For dinner they consume jellymeat, skeleton
biscuits, a fairy cake,

a portion of best carpet and a sock that is four days old.

After this feast they must be taken to a place called
walkies, which has many lamp-posts.

The Earth Hound is attached to a string so that he can be pulled along in the sitting position.

In the park, the Earthling gathers a stick from a tree
and hurls it all around.
The Earth Hound is made to fetch it.

Then the Earthling takes a bouncing sphere and flings it in the pond.

This time the Earthling has to fetch it.

On the way home, the Earth Hound rolls in the pat of a moohorn.

He arrives back at the Earth Dwelling with stinkfur
and hides under the duvet of the Earthling.

Here are some phrases I want you to learn:
"Where is Rover?"
"Is something wrong with the drains?"
"Either he goes or I do!"

Earth Hounds hate the bath of bubbles. They tuck
their wagglers between their legs and make a Wooo-
Woooooo noise.

Once clean they dry themselves on heaps of compost.

Here is a baby Earth Hound, or Houndlet, asleep in
the nocturnal footwear of an Earthling.

On the floor the Earthling has placed many
newspapers for the Houndlet to read.

That is the end of today's lesson.

If you are all good and quiet, we will visit Planet
Earth to play with a real Houndlet.

Those of you who want to bring your own pets along,
please sit at the back of the spaceship.